THE ADVENTURES OF WALTER

JANE PILGRIM
Illustrated by F. Stocks May

DERRYDALE BOOKS
New York

Walter was a large white duck who lived at Blackberry Farm. He had a strong yellow beak, and he always wore a woolen scarf around his neck because he had been hatched out on a windy day and his mother had been afraid that he would catch cold.

Every day Walter went down to the little pond beyond the farm to see what he could find in the water. "There might be something really tasty here one day," he explained to his friend Mother Hen, when she found him upside down in the pond with only his tail showing.

But Walter began to get tired of the pond. He never did find anything tasty there. He thought he would like a change. "Tell me," he asked Rusty the Sheep Dog, "where I can find some new, exciting water. I'm tired of this dull old pond." So Rusty told him about the little river that flowed through the village and on to the fields beyond.

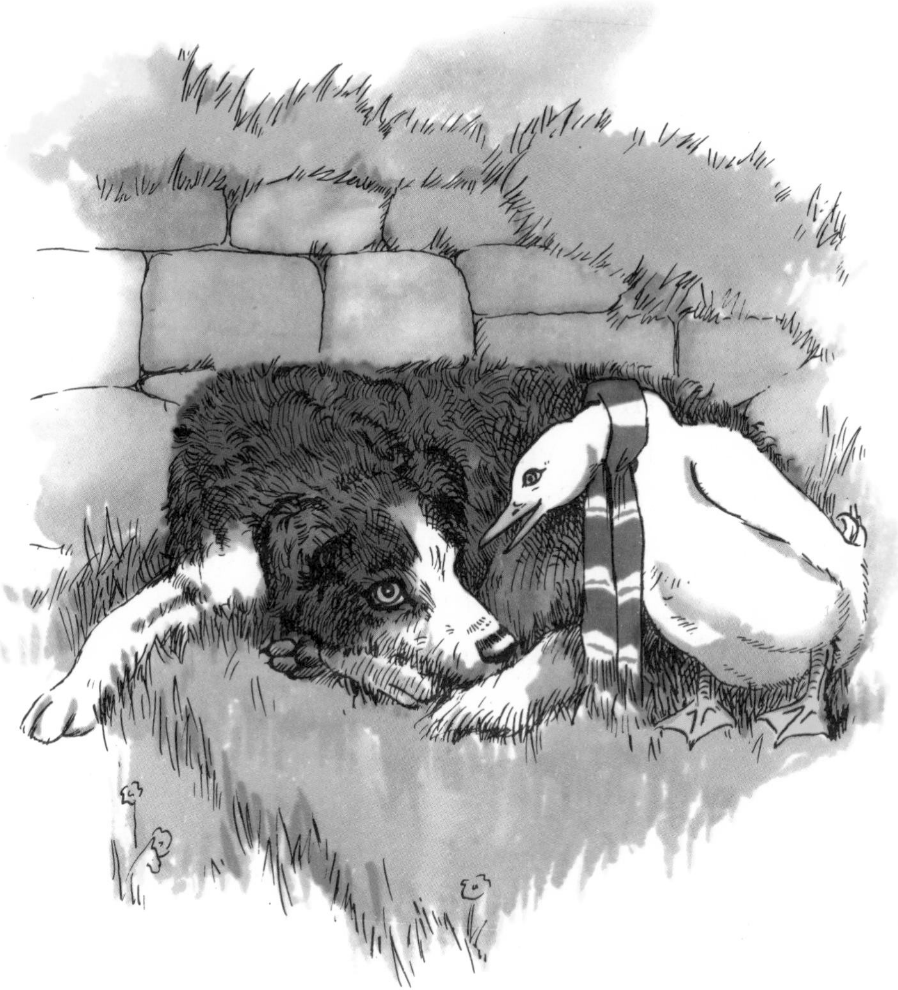

The next day Walter waddled off down the lane and past the old oak tree where Mrs. Squirrel and her daughter Hazel lived. "Good-bye, Mrs. Squirrel," he quacked, "I'm going on a journey. I'm going exploring." And on he went.

Sure enough, at the end of the lane was a little bridge, and under the bridge was a little river. Walter was delighted, and in a minute he was sailing away toward the village. "This is life," he thought. "This is better than my dull old pond." And he swam on.

When he reached the village,
Walter stopped and looked around.
An old lady threw him a crust. He
quacked his thanks and sailed on.
"This is good," he thought. "This is
better than my dull old pond." And
on he went.

But around the next corner he had a shock. There were lots of brown ducks swimming about. "Dirty ducks," Walter thought, "not clean white ducks like me," and he swam proudly on toward them. But all the brown ducks turned fiercely on him and drove him back toward the village.

"Oh dear!" sighed Walter. "Now I won't be able to see those nice green fields," And he decided to climb the bank and walk along the path. So he waddled along, humming a tune to himself. Then suddenly he saw a large Black Dog asleep across his path.

Walter was alarmed. The only dog he knew was Rusty the Sheep Dog, and he was a friendly dog. But he had heard that some dogs like to chase ducks, "I must creep around him very carefully," he thought, "without waking him up. Then I shall be all right." And he began to creep very carefully.

And he did creep very carefully, but one feather from his wing tip must have tickled the Black Dog's nose, because he suddenly opened his eyes and saw Walter.

Now the Black Dog did not know
that this was Walter Duck from
Blackberry Farm. He thought
Walter was just a lost white duck,
and that it was his duty to catch lost
white ducks and take them home.
So, in a second, he had lifted Walter
up and was carrying him carefully
in his mouth down the path
toward the village.

How Walter quacked and wriggled!
He wasn't hurt, but he was very
frightened. When would he see his
dear little pond again? Two large
tears rolled down his beak. It was
then that Rusty met them.
"Whatever are you doing with our
Walter?" he asked the Black Dog,
and the Black Dog had to put
Walter down before he could
answer.

Walter did not wait to hear the answer. He was off down the bank and into the river, swimming as fast as he could away from the village, and home to Blackberry Farm.

Rusty found him waddling down the lane past the old oak tree where Mrs. Squirrel lived. "It's all right, Walter," he told him. "That Black Dog would not have hurt you. He's a friend of mine. But next time you go exploring, I think you had better come with me, and I will look after you."

Walter was very glad to get home to his little pond again, and to find Mother Hen waiting for him. "The world is a very exciting place," he told her. "But I like Blackberry Farm best. I think I shall stay here for a long time." And he waddled happily into his own dull muddy water.

This 1987 edition is published by Derrydale Books,
distributed by Crown Publishers, Inc., 225 Park Avenue South, New York,
New York 10003, by arrangement with Hodder & Stoughton Limited

Manufactured in Spain

LIBRARY OF CONGRESS CATALOGING-IN-PUBLICATION DATA

Pilgrim, Jane.
The adventures of Walter.

(Blackberry Farm book series)
Summary: Bored with life at home, Walter the Duck sets out on an adventure
in the neighboring village.
[1. Ducks—Fiction. I. May, F. Stocks, ill.
II. Title. III. Series: Pilgrim, Jane. Blackberry Farm book series.
PZ7.P6295Ad 1987 [E] 87-9084
ISBN 0-517-64346-4
h g f e d c b a